Dear Parents,

Noah's Ark provides a wonderful opportunity to introduce one of the Bible's most powerful stories about obedience, faith, and covenant. In many ways it is a harsh illustration of how God, who loves creation, responds when that creation rejects God's love. The story reveals the consequences of what happens when humankind does not demonstrate love and caring in their daily living. It may seem severe, but it also speaks of redemption.

Noah's Ark: The Brick Bible for Kids provides amazing, child-friendly illustrations of the biblical story by utilizing a familiar toy, LEGO® building blocks, to introduce difficult subjects, such as the drowning of all the world's people by God (which is illustrated in this book). Using tools that are familiar to children can potentially help make understanding complicated issues easier.

As adults, it is difficult to understand human evil. Helping children understand evil is even more difficult. We want to protect our children from pain, hurt, tragedy, and challenges. Yet, as adults we know that the realities of life will impact our children. So how do we, as parents, reveal the realities of life in an appropriate way that doesn't traumatize, but helps them to embrace the joy and the pains of life? The story of Noah can help us to do that.

Your child might ask hard questions like "Why did God make the people drown?" or "Why would God kill people?" Depending on your child's age, your child may really be asking you if he is going to drown or if God is going to kill her. Try turning the question into a conversation about the child's safety. Reaffirm that you will be there to help your child through any difficult times in life. Explain to the child that every time he sees a rainbow in the sky, it is a reminder of God's love for all of creation.

There are a few ways to make explaining the more difficult portions of this book easier for you. Remember that communication is key. Allow your child to ask questions and listen long enough for her to come to answers that make sense to her. Be sure to always tell the truth when your child asks a difficult question, but remember that simple and brief answers are perfectly adequate. Finally, it's crucial to note that helping your child develop a love for reading the Bible by reading it together early on is important. You know your child and will be able to choose what to focus on as you read together. This may help take the focus away from areas you don't feel comfortable discussing.

In my opinion, spending time reading the Bible with a child outweighs all of the uncomfortable feelings that will inevitably arise at one time or another for both the adult and the child. A great value of the Bible is that it challenges us to think about who we are in the world and how we are to be in relationship with each other. The story of Noah and the ark is a story that can bring us closer to each other and closer to God.

—Rev. Wanda M. Lundy, Director, Doctor of Ministry Program at New York Theological Seminary

Sky Pony Press books may be purchased in bulk at special discounts for sales promotion, corporate gifts, fund-raising, or educational purposes. Special editions can also be created to specifications. For details, contact the Special Sales Department, Sky Pony Press, 307 West 36th Street, 11th Floor, New York, NY 10018 or info@skyhorsepublishing.com.

Sky Pony® is a registered trademark of Skyhorse Publishing, Inc.®, a Delaware corporation.

Visit our website at www.skyponypress.com.

10 9 8 7 6 5 4 3 2 1

Manufactured in Canada, November 2014
This product conforms to CPSIA 2008

Paperback ISBN: 978-1-63450-054-8

Library of Congress has catalogued the hardcover edition as follows:

Smith, Brendan Powell.
 Noah's ark : the brick Bible for kids / Brendan Powell Smith.
    p. cm.
 ISBN 978-1-61608-737-1 (hardcover : alk. paper)
1. Noah (Biblical figure)--Juvenile literature. 2. Noah's ark--Juvenile literature. 3. Deluge--Juvenile literature. 4. LEGO toys--Juvenile literature. I. Title.
 BS580.N6S65 2012
 222'.1109505--dc23

                              2011052514

Editor: Julie Matysik
Designer: Brian Peterson
Production Manager: Abigail Gehring

Noah's Ark
THE BRICK BIBLE for Kids

Brendan Powell Smith

Sky Pony Press
New York

God looked at the world and saw that all the people were very bad.

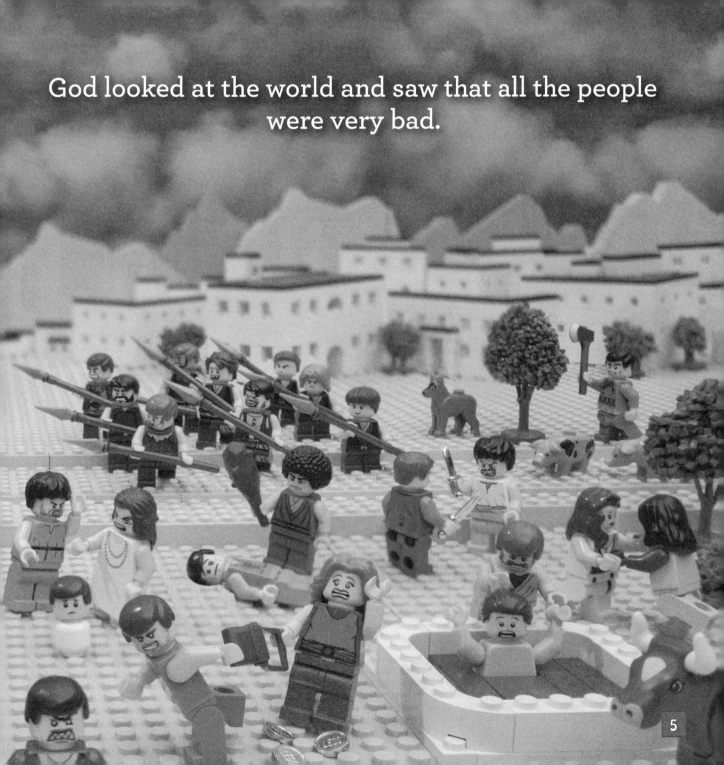

God decided He would wash away all the people and animals of the world with a giant flood.

Now, in all the world, there was only one good person. His name was Noah. Noah had a wife and three sons.

God told Noah to build a big boat called an ark to keep his family safe from the flood.

God told Noah to take two of every kind of animal
in the world and put them on the ark to keep
them safe.

So Noah went out and gathered two of every kind
of farm animal.

And two of every kind of wild animal.

He gathered two of every type of bird, both big and small.

And two of every living thing that creeps along the ground.

God also told Noah to bring aboard the ark all the
kinds of food that all the different animals eat.

All the animals entered the ark in pairs.

Finally, God told Noah to bring his family into the ark with him and God shut the doors.

Then God began to flood the world. Water burst up out of the ground and rain poured down from the sky.

The water rose so high that the ark Noah built was lifted off the ground.

It rained for forty days and forty nights. The water rose so high that even the tallest mountains were covered.

Finally the rain stopped and the ark floated on top of the waters.

Months passed and Noah's family stayed inside the ark and fed all the animals.

Then God remembered Noah and lowered the waters. The ark came to rest on top of a mountain.

Noah opened the window of the ark and released a dove. The dove returned to Noah with a branch from an olive tree in its beak.

Then God told Noah it was time for his family and the animals to come out from the ark.

Noah was thankful to God, so he built an altar and
made an offering.

God was pleased and promised Noah he would
never again drown all the people and animals
of the world with a flood.

God put a rainbow in the sky, and told Noah that whenever a rainbow appears, He would remember that promise.

Activity!

Can you find these ten brick pieces in the book?
On which page does each appear?
The answers are below.

A.

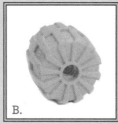
B.

C.

D.

E.

F.

G.

H.

I.

J.

Answer key:

A: pp.8 and 9, B: p.22, C: p.7, D: p.24, E: p.6, F: p.6, G: p.28, H: p.19, I: p.12, J: pp.15 and 24